Kumkum Malhotra

Preti Taneja

Gatehouse Press

Published by
Gatehouse Press Limited
90 Earlham Road
Norwich NR2 3HA
www.gatehousepress.com

ISBN 978-0-9928573-6-3

About the *New Fictions* Pamphlets

The *New Fictions* pamphlets from Gatehouse Press is a series that aims to publish the best new long-form short fiction. Between two and four entries are selected from an open submission process in the 4th quarter of each year; we aim to give a platform both to new writers and to more experienced writers who explore the limits of the short fiction and novella genres. All Gatehouse staff are volunteers, and all profits go back into publishing. For more information, including how to submit work for the current year of the project, see our website: http://www.gatehousepress.com

Body text set in Garamond; titles in Day Roman. Used under licence.

Special thanks to Lee Seaman, James Higham and Natty Peterkin

Cover illustrations by Natty Peterkin, nattypeterkin.tumblr.com
Cover design by Norwich Designer
Printed and bound in the UK

Kumkum Malhotra

I

From her window Kumkum can see : baby Madhu on the swing and Nunni running in circles with her dolly in her hand. Up and down and round and round. Since Madhu arrived they play like this – one circling the other like sun and earth. Madhu is smiling, that is good, that means she is enjoying; she is safe. But how many times has she told Nunni not to run! The mitti is dry in the yard – if she falls she will cry, worse, she will tear her salwar and there is no time for such accidents tonight. Where is Ashish? Kumkum stands on tiptoe in her blouse and petticoat, using the thin cotton curtain as a sari. Ashish and his gang are huddled in the outer corner as if they are making a secret : she cranes and twists but cannot see.

It is nothing. She must dress. She forgets the children and turns with the dust motes caught in the late light, back to herself in the full-length mirror, and her preparations for the evening ahead.

One, two. With what careful balance she slips each foot into its high-heeled sandal! Tonight the family will be together for the first time in three years. Three brothers, three wives, three children. As the wife of Shalu, middle brother, Kumkum wants to look her best. As the wife of Shalu, the middle brother whose business is failing, she wants it particularly. She puts four hairgrips, black ridged and designed to be invisible, between her lips, raises her arms and winds her hair up and back, securing it with jabs. Once – the dinner will be at Raviji and Seemaji's house. Twice – she and Shalu have not been invited to visit them for so long. Thrice – even so, the distance between the houses is no more than the diameter of New Delhi. Fourth – the fourth is not needed, she places it back into its compartment in the drawer.

From the top of the cupboard she takes her mother's wooden jewellery box; there are three pieces inside. She makes a pain face as she screws in her grandmother's diamond studs. They glint in her ears : two bright chips of stars. She fastens her one necklace : her wedding mangal sutra. She closes the lid on her Dādāji's old watch – strap frayed but face and hands always ready for business – and stores the box away.

She leans into the mirror to paint lipstick, it smells of old roses and wax. This was a gift from Seemaji two years back and has not ever been used. Her hand is unsteady with the shape of it; she has to wipe off the colour and do it again. She leans forwards and must brace her hips on the edge of the dresser. She knocks her powder and a white cloud puffs into the air then settles, turning her brown skin grey.

The scrunched, spent tubes of *Fair and Lovely* lie on her table with her brush, her rollers and her polish, her nail scissors still caught with hairs from Shalu's beard. She will have to clean this before she goes out. Shalu likes the house in tiptop order always. Especially now Vivek and Kiran have come from London, all the way from London. And baby Madhu on her first trip home. Staying with her and Shalu and Ashish and Nunni in a part of the city where cows still roam in the lanes. Dust from the street laps at her door, everyday she wipes with a damp cloth the plastic flowers that occupy her mother's cut-glass vases. Despite all of this, their London family are basing here, and not with Raviji and Seemaji.

Kumkum begins to wind and pleat her sari, looking at herself in the mirror and not down at her hands. She tucks the stiff silk into her petticoat, stands up straight. She slides her fingers between her sari pleats and shakes hard, so they fall correctly to her carefully painted toenails, and flips the pullu over her shoulder, turning to see how it falls down her back.

Shalu says he has a 'special bond' with his younger brother and that is the reason for their choice. This morning when she was on her haunches doing the paunachha on the bathroom floor after her husband's bath, he told her, 'Ya, a special bond. And you should get to know Kiran more also. She is a good wife. And time for the children to meet their cousin from London.' He finished applying his hair oil and wiped his hands across his chest. He only had a towel covering the rest.

Kumkum averted her eyes. She thought about the gifts that had appeared from their cases, whisky for Shalu and too-small clothes for the children who have grown so much. For her : nuggets of biscuit in a round red tin, the words *St Michael* lettered in gold on the top. She should take them to the dinner tonight, she knows, and share them. But Seemaji does go to London. She smooths her sari across her breasts and does not pin it. Unlike her older sister-in-law, she can hold it up with her posture alone.

She stands, checking with critical eyes different parts of herself in the mirror.

Mouth : lined around the edges but not so much. Hair : not a grey although it falls from her head all day as if she has a hundred new strands growing each time. Elbows : smooth. Because they always show a woman's age she looks after them particularly. Stomach : she stands straighter. Even though she is only twenty-eight, ten years of marriage, two children and a husband with a failing business make things difficult. Shalu : this morning he stopped his spitting, gargling, nasal clearing to ask her to be sure to look nice this evening.

Behind her head the sun is reflected, an egg cracked through the smog, dripping gold over the telegraph wires. She is lulled by the last of the light in the room, gifting her body its glow. Could she still be a bride? Outside, the sky blushes pink. She can hear the children's voices, distant from the yard.

What can't Kumkum see? Ashish gripping Nunni by the root of her plait. 'Go get Madhu, na,' he says, because he is in charge of the gang. He does not look at his sister when he talks, she is just his sister; and his eyes are fixed on his boys, protecting their new find.

'Madhu is swinging, she is just a baby, you should leave her, Ashish,' Nunni says.

Ashish grabs on her upper arm. 'Come on do what I tell you, you know Mamma says you have to listen to your elders.' He squeezes her; he's told her to go but he's not going to let her, he's going to make her look at the thing on the ground with him. In his other hand he is holding a stick.

'Stupid she did not mean elder brothers.' Nunni wrestles away from Ashish and runs through the wrought iron gate of the yard to where cousin Madhu is swinging on the old plank swing, and singing to herself.

'What are you singing, Madhu baby?' Since Madhu arrived at their house with Kiran Aunty From London, Nunni isn't the youngest any more. Yesterday, when her Papa called her 'baby' she told him so.

Madhu smiles at her, shakes her head and kicks her legs; Nunni goes behind and pushes so the swing soars over the dusty yard. When it hangs for a second, high in the air, Nunni sees Madhu stretching her neck to call to Ashish and the boys by the gate. When she swoops down low, Nunni holds out her arms and smiles and waves. Up high Madhu goes – down low again, and the sun curling over the lip of the roof gets in Nunni's eyes.

'Jump!' she shouts, she drops her dolly so she is ready –

'Catch me!' shouts Madhu, and launches herself at her cousin.

Nunni is only six to Madhu's four, she is too small for this, or Madhu is too big. With two high screams, both girls fall back into the dirt, Nunni's yellow churidar tears at the knee and Madhu's dress comes over her head. Madhu's kutchas are showing, the same pink as her dress; there's a hoo-ha from the boys at the gate and Nunni struggles to her feet. But the boys aren't looking at them; they're still poke-poking at something she cannot see. She turns and stares down at Madhu. The little girl stares back at her. Blood is seeping from her knee, her forehead. Dark, like Mamma's pot of nail polish : Special Occasion. Nunni fingers her knee but forces tears back as Madhu's eyes begin to fill. Why doesn't the stupid baby get up? Nunni bends and pulls Madhu's dress down to cover her.

'You don't show your kutchas it's not London, OK?' she says, and runs towards the house.

Kumkum catches her at the screen door and wheels her by the shoulders back towards Madhu lying still in the yard, staring at the sky. The swing is swinging, just missing Madhu's head. Kumkum's sari crumples in the dirt as she kneels to gather her niece into her arms. Praying and muttering, she checks Madhu is not seriously hurt. She smells of mitti and tutti. Kumkum bites her lip and tastes roses and wax; sweat begins to make her khol run. A sick feeling closes her throat at the thought of facing her husband, her brother and sister-in-law and telling them that Madhu got hurt when she was supposed to be taking care. It will not matter that she was actually getting herself ready for them coming home; that she wanted to look like a woman in the first year of marriage just for tonight. She has sacrificed Madhu for her vanity.

She picks the little girl up and sets her on her feet, brushing her frilly dress down. 'OK, OK, meri jaan,' she croons, and Madhu starts to cry. 'Come now, don't cry Madhu, good girl, hain? Good girl.' She wipes at Madhu's face with the fall of her sari; Madhu grips and it pulls tighter, and Kumkum is almost dragged sideways into the dirt. 'See? Silly Kumkum Chachī nearly fell also!'

Nunni giggles then falls quiet.

'Go inside Nunni, I know this was you being naughty, just wait I'll tell Papa – go and change your salwar. Tearing your clothes all the time.' As she speaks to her daughter her hands are busy with Madhu, wiping, checking, soothing, smoothing : her dark red nails and ringed fingers catch in the lace of the little girl's dress. She watches Nunni run inside and knows she will have to be placated with a sweet jelabi and hot milk later. In fact, both these girls could do with that. Ashish also. She stands. Ashish is ten years old. Why was he not taking care of his sister and his cousin while she was busy inside?

'Ashish!' she calls in her 'I'm going to tell Papa' voice. The group of boys by the gate nudge each other to mute and frozen. 'Ashish, come inside now. Don't make me come there.'

She waits for her son to leave the group. Still he does not move. Beside her Madhu is standing on her own, but when Kumkum tries to let go of her hand, the little girl clings on even tighter, saying nothing.

'Come on then, let's see what these naughty boys are doing.' Her sari is already dirty; she heaves Madhu up into her arms. She feels the small body become sticky and relax. A tickly little head goes onto her shoulder; wetness from Madhu's face glues it to the sweat on Kumkum's neck.

Kumkum carries her over to the pack of boys. 'Out of the way, what is this business?' She will have to put Madhu down to grab a boy and move him; or use the little girl to break the circle. 'Move,' she says. The boys shift so she can see.

And then she wishes she couldn't. That she hadn't come over, or even come out of the house.

In the middle of the circle of boys is a skull. Flesh still clings to it in red, rotting clumps. Maggots and flies crawl around its eye sockets and from the place where its horns sprout on either side. Clean picked patches of bone show through like bald spots. Kumkum feels her hot sweat run cold. She thinks it is a cow's skull, she does not want Madhu to see it; she holds the child's head into her neck. It cannot be a cow : the neighbourhood is quiet, has been even since last year. No, it cannot be a cow, it can't be, no. It's a dog, it's a bison, it's a mutton, it's a goat; it's

12

just been kicked here by accident of course. But nothing has died and rotted here, she would have seen it over days. It is not a cow, but still, still : someone has left this thing for her family to find.

Someone must have wanted to insult them. Someone against Shalu? Someone maybe thinks she is not visiting the temple enough, that her children are running too wild. Someone always has something to say. She licks her dry lips. She can almost see a tongue lolling from the skull's half jaw : thirsting. But the thing is silent, its tongue long gone – swallowed by what she can't imagine. Its eyes don't see and yet the sockets are alive; they are buzzing with life.

Kumkum tries to look away but the shock of death freezes her gaze. The cow's fly eyes stare back at her in their teeming hundreds. She cannot give up the idea that it is a cow, though she knows it must not be. Too small, too angled. It seems to stare at her, it knows everything she has never told anyone, everything that is about to come to her. It will not provide milk, or give up its hide; it is past its usefulness. She cannot stop the sickness rising from just below where her petticoat too tightly bisects her waist. Her arms go slack; she feels Madhu tumble down her body and thump to the ground, grabbing the front of her sari as she does so, pulling the silk free from the petticoat. The pleats fall out, fan open and cover the child. Madhu scrabbles for light, she starts to wail; Kumkum bends over, trying to gather the material in her arms and pick up Madhu and stop looking at the skull. She cannot free her. Madhu's fat little hands claw the sari from her, she leans forward, a fly jumps from the cow's stunted horn and lands on the baby's cheek, feeding on the sweet sweat from Kumkum's neck and on Madhu's salty tears. Madhu's

13

hand reaches and touches the rotten flesh and comes back to her face to rub at the fly tickle, there is blood on her cheek from her hand, her wails become screams; she sounds like a calf being slaughtered.

Kumkum feels the swinging of the world around her, and the sun, and the eyes of the boys on her, and the crying of the baby, the boys shouting, No!, and Move the thing! the yard wall becomes a white line of heat across her vision; the swing curves back and forth; its creaking laughs at her, 'hai hai!' She reaches out and lets go of all the fabric in her hands. Her sari is falling off her all over the ground, and she bends down and slaps the fly off Madhu's face. Slaps as hard as she can.

The little girl goes backwards in the dust, wrenching the last pleats of Kumkum's sari free and popping a hook from the eyes on her blouse. Madhu screams even harder as the pool of silk falls on her again, starts to kick out : as Kumkum grabs her, Madhu catches her in the side of her breast with her fist. Kumkum tries to lift Madhu, the weight of her bound hair falls sideways. Madhu clutches and pulls, the grips give, the hair loosens and falls with a thousand whispers down Kumkum's back.

Bent over in her petticoat and gaping blouse with the child screaming into her ear, Kumkum shifts her neck upwards. Her eyes rake the group of boys, trying to shame them into looking away. They meet her with the stares of men seeing a woman for the first time. They are not boys, not sons. They stare at the ends of her hair, licking down her skin; they stare at her breasts, they don't look away. They stare blankly, as the cow stares up at her from the ground. Ashish himself stares at her, her own son. 'Ma!' comes a shout. Kumkum looks up and back to see Nunni on the terrace; she must be standing on a chair so

14

she can see. Can see her mother exposed in the street. See her slapped cousin covered in blood.

The sound of a car horn drowns out Nunni's cries. Kumkum takes Madhu by one hand, her sari in the other hand, and stands up. The boys scatter down the lane to their mothers. Ashish pushes past her and runs inside. Nunni's head disappears from the terrace. Kumkum is left half-naked in the street, a bloody skull at her feet, a child marked red and screaming next to her, as her husband and her in-laws arrive home.

'Did Mummy hit Madhu?' Raviji has Ashish and Nunni sitting side by side on the leather sofa in the brightly lit lounge. Raviji stands in front of them, blocking them from Kumkum's view. Shalu sits in the armchair in the corner, whisky in his hand, watching his older brother address his children.

Kumkum in the hallway : her fingers pull at her plait. Strands of hair come loose and she twists them around her middle finger tip until it bulges blue. From the marble floors to the glass tables, everything in this apartment is gleaming, each surface reflecting the other so there is nowhere for eyes to rest.

In the guest bedroom Madhu and Kiran are being comforted and settled by Seemaji. 'Come Kiran, don't worry,' says Seemaji. 'We will get Ashish and Nunni here to play with Madhu. We always love to have children in the house. And I told you then that you would be better off staying here. We have more space, it is better you keep here with us,' she says.

Their suitcases, Madhu's stroller, their shopping from this day, all spills from the bags on the floor around them. Kumkum

15

goes in and tries to put her hands on Kiran but her sister-in-law turns her shoulder and Seemaji shakes her head.

So she goes into the kitchen and pushes the maid out of the way. She picks up the cākū and reaches for the onions; she can cut salad at least. But she can hear Raviji questioning the children and the onion stays whole in her hand.

'Ashish, did Mummy hit Madhu?' Raviji sounds gentle, almost teasing.

She has already told them what happened. What is the need for this now?

'Ashish, just tell me beta, what happened?' Raviji says again, his voice like a knife introducing itself politely to the soft sweet skin of a plum.

Ashish's voice is spiked with fear. 'Chachaji,' he says. 'I don't know.'

'Come Ashish, you were standing there, no? Come, tell me. Or maybe Nunni will remember. Nunni, did Mummy hit Madhu? Answer me beti, and nothing will happen. More sweet jelabi for you.'

'Yes, Chachaji,' says Nunni. 'But –'

'What. She hits you also?'

'No, but – '

'Then just answer my question, good girl.'

'Chachaji,' says Nunni. 'The answer to your question is yes. Mummy hit Madhu baby.'

In the kitchen, Kumkum's hands are still, open, resting on the cutting board.

'And what else, huh? Did she take her sari off in the road? Ashish?'

16

'No! I think Mummy dropped Madhu by mistake, and she pulled her sari off.'

Kumkum smiles. Her son always has to be so correct. Her palms press together : a silent clap, a prayer.

'Tell the truth beta,' Raviji says. 'You're a strong man now, your cousin-sister got hurt. We want to help your Mummy to look after you properly. Tell me slowly. Did Mummy drop Madhu baby?'

Two voices: 'Yes'.

'Was Mummy wearing her sari?'

Two voices: 'Yes'.

'And did Mummy hit Madhu?'

Two voices: 'Yes'.

'And was Mummy wearing her sari all the time?'

Two voices: 'No, Chachaji'.

'OK. Good children. Rupa!'

The maid scuttles past Kumkum into the lounge.

'Yes, Sahib?'

'Put on cartoons in the TV room, give these children dinner there, make them sleep after.'

She hears the children unstick themselves from the leather sofa. They follow Rupa into the inner room. The TV starts, and is silenced as Raviji shuts the dividing door

On the way home, Shalu and Kumkum say nothing. It is late, and around the ring-road huge lorries chase each other, sleek cars with black windows glide by. Their own white Maruti does not belong here at this hour. Kumkum twists against the seatbelt to check the backseat : Ashish and Nunni are asleep.

They turn into the enclave and reach home. Kumkum gets out of the car. She unlocks the gate and stands back as her husband drives through. She locks it behind him. She goes to the front door and opens the padlock, draws the bolt back, opens the door. A car door slams, and then again, and again. She goes to help. Instead of waiting for her, Shalu is walking towards the house. Nunni is locked in his arms, Ashish stumbles with sleep in front of them. Shalu guides his son past Kumkum and she watches as they carry on up the stairs. Nunni, facing her mother over her father's shoulder, does not wake up.

Kumkum undresses in the dark. She takes off her makeup and leaves her salwar kameeze, her chunni, her bra and panties neatly folded, even though they are dirty and need to be washed. Her jewellery placed back in the wooden casket. Naked, she steps into the bathroom, to dunk and splash ice-cold water from the bucket onto her body until goosebumps come. She puts on her nightgown and buttons it up. Slips into bed beside Shalu's humped back and lies open-eyed in the dark.

Vivek and Kiran and little Madhu are leaving back to London. Seemaji's driver is taking them to the flight. They stop only for an on-the-way-to-the-airport-tea-and-snacks goodbye at Shalu's house. It is just before Ashish and Nunni get home from school.

'Such a shame,' says Seemaji, as delicately as the edible gold leaf adorning her burfi, 'that Ashish goes to the local school, when we have so many topflight schools to really teach children what is what?' All agree. 'And such a shame,' she continues, 'that the local children are such a raggle-taggle! If it were my daughter, I would worry.' All agree. 'We are always thinking about how to support Nunni in her growing up. And then also,' she says, as she considers the sweet burfi she is eating as if it is a real gold biscuit, 'we know you want the best for the children Shaluji.' Doesn't Shalu want Ashish to grow big and strong? Go to college in USA? Come back and get a good job? Doesn't Shalu want Nunni to be brought up properly, with other good girls, and get a good Delhi University degree and make a good marriage and both to be the true son and daughter to their Uncleji and Auntieji and Daddyji?

'Of course, Sisterji,' says Shalu. 'But the business, my health; what can we do? We are not blessed with success like you and Raviji.'

Putting down her burfi as if she were placing a bet on Diwali, Seemaji says, 'We could help. And if you want Nunni to go to a good Delhi school, of course she could live with her Uncleji and Aunt.'

Shalu smiles. Kumkum can't move. She keeps her eyes on the burfi, pale flat diamonds piled carelessly on her flower-patterned wedding set. Bone china. Naturally prone to break.

Into the silence, Seemaji says, 'No, no, don't need to say any thank-you. You are our only family. We should have done it sooner only. But you know, my diabetes.' As she speaks, she licks her lips, her fingers select another diamond, bites half away.

Kumkum finally moves : to sit on her own, everyday hands. Bad behaviour for a mother of two and ten years married. Where are her rings? One sold, one eaten by Nunni when she was a baby and gone down the toilet hole before it could be

19

rescued. You cannot catch something coming out of a child when you are holding that child streaming over the pot. She feels a laugh rising in her, and coughs.

Seemaji raises an eyebrow at her, waiting for more tea to be poured. But Kumkum has no hands. Kiran reaches in and pours instead. She does not look at Kumkum. Then Seemaji says, 'It's getting late, time to go.' The party leaves for the airport; the tea goes cold.

Then Ashish comes home with a black eye and crying. He does not speak to his mother, has not since the dinner.

When Shalu comes to bed, he stands over his wife, looking down at her : her nightie buttoned, her hair braided, her eyes cast down. 'My son is not the captain of his class anymore, my wife,' he says.

She does not reply. She feels a pain in her breasts and places her hand on the left one, kneading it as her husband speaks.

'Because his teacherji's son saw you naked in the street only, screaming and slapping the baby.' Shalu pauses, as if expecting her to jump up and re-enact the scene for him, take off her nightie and do it there, in the middle of the room so he can slap her right back. She does not raise her eyes.

'My son. His own classmates don't respect him anymore.' Shalu makes a fist and punches the air in front of him.

Her hand stops moving on her breast. Her husband keeps looking at her. She feels her eyes have become sightless as if the sockets are empty, and remembers the buzzing life that feeds on decay. What can she reply? Handless, eyeless and tongueless, too.

20

The children depart for their new lives in too-big clothes and new shoes for their new school, and the inside of the house takes on a strange character. In a city where there is no dark, no quiet and no solitude, Kumkum discovers all three. Her hair begins to fall out in fists : soon the soft skinned scalp will show, no matter how much she tries to hide it. She begins to wear her chuni always over her head.

She grew up with brothers and sisters, now scattered across the world like pearls from a broken necklace. Yes, the old string is rotten and the knots undone. No siblings, no friends – she once had neighbours but since the dinner day, the women all seem to look at her strangely, and keep their children from the house with the swing in the yard. She knows what they say, that she is nothing without her daughter and even less without her son.

Kumkum still serves her husband's dinner every day, but as night falls they play hunt and catch through the house, Shalu stalking Kumkum's shadow, Kumkum leaving each room just as he enters it, until he retires alone. She has taken to sleeping in Ashish's bed, and he does not follow her there.

But one day he does. She opens her eyes in a bright morning to see : her husband standing over her again. She reaches for her chuni, drapes it over her head and tucks it under her chin. Shalu clears his throat. He tells her that he has sold the failing business to a Bombay investor who isn't going to keep it running, but wants the land to build on. He invested the money, he says, to pay for Nunni one day. He pets his paunch as he speaks. His eyes stare at some point by her feet. 'And so my dear wife,' he says, 'we must empty this room. No more sleeping here.'

This time Kumkum does raise her eyes, and this time it is Shalu who keeps his cast down. She sees his lip, the beads of sweat.

He replies as if she has spoken. 'The children don't need these things now. And you can't keep sleeping here, Kumkum, what is the matter with you?' The sweat quickens as his voice becomes firmer, louder. 'And don't tell me "No,"' he says. 'You come back to our room and sleep properly. I have made arrangements – this room will go for tenancy.' He speaks as if he is seeking his mother's breast, or reaching for another hot roti at dinnertime – the certainty that what he wants will be his, for that is the right order of things. Then he leaves her, and she does not follow. It is her last night in the children's room.

II

From her window, Kumkum can see : a bobbed-blonde head, long ripped-jeans legs and a pair of old leather chapals on two dirty white feet. A white kurta arm pulls a sleeping roll and a backpack the size of a small child from the auto, a hand pays the driver then the parts all seem to turn at different moments. Kumkum draws back into the shadows of the room. She steps forward again to look, her hand re-tucks her chunni under her chin. She is met with a dark-eyed camera obscuring the girl's face. A long lens points straight at her from below and she turns all the way back, runs down the stairs and opens the screen door, shading her eyes from the light. As her sight adjusts, she sees the dirty feet carry the blue jeans, backpack, white kurta and blonde hair through the gate, past the old swing and up to the door. Turquoise eyes smile at Kumkum. The pink mouth speaks. 'Hello. I'm Anya,' it says. 'I'm here.'

Anya is messy. Her Hindi is basic and she cannot eat with one hand. She smokes and she wears men's clothes. Kumkum wants to ask – what happened to the man whose loose pyjamas you lounge in while you draw everything, from every angle in the house? What about the man (fatter than the first) whose white vests show your underarms and front and back, and under which you only wear your own coloured vest? And who is missing the stars-and-stripes undershorts with the front opening? Anya wears them to sleep in and to do PE in her room each morning. How did you come to own them?

24

When she's sketching, Kumkum watches her, until Anya offers to show her, and Kumkum says, 'No, no.' When she's cooking, Anya talks to her, telling her about the Indian boyfriend she met at university in the States and thought she loved, but who didn't survive Anya's all-consuming passion for art, spicy food and something she calls 'Tantra'.

'He didn't like me doing it when he just wanted to have sex,' Anya says. 'He was a real, you know : in and out and poke and smoke.'

Kumkum pauses in her kneading of the chapatti dough, which is perfectly giving and perfectly resistant under her fist. 'Kya?' she says, 'kya bōla?'

'You know, Kumkum... making love.'

'Chi! What a world you come from Anya,' says Kumkum. She re-tucks her chunni under her chin. Her kneading resumes.

'Hey, liven up, Sisterji,' says Anya with a smile and a shrug. 'It's 1993.'

Kumkum pinches a piece of the tender dough, and rolls it into a ball. She flattens it with her palm on the counter and begins to roll it out. Anya laughs, and Kumkum hunches over the stove.

Anya might come in and go out but always she leaves a trail of things around the house. Her scarves and her bangles, bought one day and shown off with delight and discarded the next. Cloth bags and cushion covers she drapes on her bed and then leaves to fade in the sun. In one morning she might change her mind twice or thrice about her clothes or the colour of her nails. Yet some things she is careful with. A family of painted Kashmiri boxes comes one out of the other. Anya sets those up on the shelf by the window, where

Ashish used to keep his miniature American car collection on show.

One day she sits and watches Anya use tweezers to take out her eyebrow hairs; the face she makes is so funny. The next day Kumkum shows her to the market and introduces her to the parlour where, on some occasions, she has gone for threading. Anya takes to having it each second week. Kumkum walks with her and waits. After the threading there is coconut water, which they drink standing at the stand with straws sticking straight from boreholes in the shells. The market vālē stare and so do others. It is she, not Anya, who attracts more of their eyes. Each time someone looks Anya waits until they have passed by and then makes a face and quickly mimics two steps of their walk, a tall blonde Charlie Chaplin in the market kutchra. Always this is followed by a glance at Kumkum, a raised eyebrow, before her face becomes serious again.

One deep monsoon day she is doing laundry. Anya insists on helping, and they kneel in the dirty clothes, sheets and so on, sorting into piles by size and colour. Anya has never asked why they don't send the piles to the dhobi, why there isn't even a wash girl to come in and help Kumkum pump the waterpump and beat the clothes against the stone in the back courtyard, or a sweeper to wash the carbolic suds down the corner drain. Nor does she send her own clothes outside. Instead, with the rain drumming down, they work together in silence, every now and then smiling as their hands meet in the clothes.

Then Anya picks up a pair of Shalu's Y-front underpants. She sticks her littlest finger through the opening and wiggles it at Kumkum. 'Oh please, Anya,' Anya says, wiggling and giggling. 'Don't tell my mummy!' Kumkum raises herself high on her knees, she cocks her chin, her eyebrow and her hip, acting Sri Devi. 'Chi!' she says, flicking a handkerchief. 'What do you call that? Your…pencil?' and she falls forward laughing. Anya catches her and they clutch each other trying to get their breath.

Anya says 'Kumkum! You are laughing! I did it!' and more mirth comes from them, frothy as the suds that clean the clothes. As Kumkum takes the underpants from Anya they laugh even harder.

Then Anya tries to speak. She says, 'bus… Mr India… blood… my jeans.' She covers her face and falls forward. Holding her, kneeling on the floor among the dirty washing, Kumkum rocks Anya while she cries.

The door opens, and Ashish stands in the frame. An older Ashish, not ten anymore, but thirteen. Her skinny, tall boy – an exclamation mark in his school uniform and cap. He keeps his hand on the door and stares at Anya. Behind him in the shadows, Kumkum waits with her hand on her son's shoulder, as if to pull him back or push him forward. She wonders if her son has ever been this close to an Angrezi woman before.

Anya is hunched over a sketchpad, hands moving. Her face is obscured under the light fall of her hair; as pale as Amul Unsalted. 'Hello,' she says.

'Sorry to disturb, Anya, I told to him not to come up here,' Kumkum says.

Anya looks up. Her blue eyes sweep over Ashish and seem to grow wider for a second. 'Who are you?'

'Hello. I am Ashish,' he blurts. 'This is my room.'

And now Anya puts down her sketchpad. She was drawing her own foot. She sits up fully straight. 'Do you pay for this room Ashish? Have you come to claim it?' She is smiling. She pushes her hand through the butter gold hair as if spreading it from her face. She regards the boy.

'Forgive him, Anya.' Kumkum prods Ashish and he steps forward sharply at her touch. 'He just came for the afternoon only, after such a long time. Before he went to school, he slept here.'

'I am Ashish,' says Ashish again, in his new School Captain voice. He bows to Anya. 'Madam.'

Anya laughs and claps her hands. 'Well,' she says. 'Since this was your room, I thank you for renting it to me. Sir.'

'Are you an artist?' asks Ashish.

'No. I'm a photographer. And India is my picture.' Anya holds out her sketchbook to Ashish. 'Look.'

As Kumkum watches, he flips a leaf. The sketch of Anya's foot gives way to mounted photo shots of a pink frilled little girl holding her mother's hand at the bus stop near their enclave, of shoeless boys playing football in the enclave garden, of a cow stopping the traffic, its milky gaze unfocused despite the hordes of people around it, the cars, the lorries, the scooters, the rickshaws. It looks beyond, locking eyes with the camera for the split second it took Anya to press the button.

'Art will not make India great,' says Ashish, handing the sketchbook back.

Anya sits up straighter. 'Kumkum,' she says, 'His voice is Dartington cut crystal, with a Made in India stamp on it!'

'Come Ashish, we have disturbed Anya enough.' She ushers Ashish in front of her and quietly closes the door on Anya's silent questions. Outside, the car is waiting to take Ashish back to his Aunt and Uncleji's house, and when it pulls away he does not look back.

Kumkum goes to the kitchen. It is dark in the house : the walls are thick, the windows small. Standing on a step stool, she reaches above the kitchen cupboard and lifts down the tray that carries her mandir. The bronzed, kneeling Hanuman is a cold weight in her hand. He gives no response as she bends to place him on the counter. She reaches up again and draws back the curtain that hides the cupboard door. From the back of the cupboard comes a circular tin box. *St Michael.* She climbs down the ladder, cradling the tin. At the table she opens it. Inside : Nunni's cloth dolly, washed and put away. Ashish's school reports. A few photos of them as babies. A cough interrupts her – Anya is standing there, her face obscured by her camera. There is a single click. The camera is lowered. Anya isn't smiling.

She crosses the kitchen towards Kumkum, and sits down slowly, firmly, the judge in the court of one. 'You have a son. Kumkum. How come you never told me you have a son?' She reaches out and tries to pull the box towards her. Kumkum will not let it go. For a moment it is locked between them, then Kumkum sits back and Anya hugs it to her, as if it is her prize, her child.

'Anya. Since you came here we have been good friends, no?' Kumkum does not look at Anya, instead her hands inch across the table, back towards the tin.

'Who is this?' Anya holds up a picture of Nunni snapped with her dolly on her first day of elementary school. 'Some niece you don't see much? Or do you have a daughter too?'

Kumkum's hand goes to her mouth. Anya says, 'My fucking God. You do, don't you? Kumkum, friends tell each other things. Friends trust each other.'

Anya gets up. She crosses behind Kumkum and reaches out to pull Kumkum's chunni from her head. A brown hand clasps a white, then lets go. Anya pulls, and reveals what in three years she has never properly been invited to see : the bald crown of her friend's hairless head.

'What did he do?' Anya kneels by Kumkum's chair. The two women face each other. Kumkum stiff in her dark salwar kameeze, her chunni draped around her neck. Anya in her light cotton kurta; her loose pyjama; butter-blond skimming her knees. She lifts the camera again and takes picture after picture, clickclickclickclickclick.

Kumkum draws her chunni back over her scalp. 'Anya you're just a girl,' she says.

'You and me are the same age,' replies Anya. She stands and takes off the camera. Gets out her cigarettes, lights one. 'Kumkum. Please. Tell me what happened. I want to help.'

Kumkum slides from her chair, crosses to the cupboard and returns to the table. She places an ashtray in front of Anya. 'Nothing happened. Their aunt and uncle pay for them to go to school. Nunni,' she falters, then continues, 'is here in Delhi.

Ashish studies in school in Deradhun, about six hours from here by train.'

'Your daughter goes to school in Delhi and she never comes home? How old is she? You don't see her?'

'Ten. She lives with her aunt and uncle. It's better for her, only.'

Anya takes a final suck and stubs the cigarette out. 'Right. Fine. If you won't tell me why you haven't seen your ten-year-old daughter since she was six – six! Don't. I'll get it out of Shalu in the lounge tonight.' She mimes the shaking of a bottle to her mouth. She drinks with him sometimes, sitting up late in the lounge. In the morning she complains, with her hand to her head, that the bare light from the bulb has given her a headache, that there should be more cushions, that the room is not cosy enough to be called a lounge. 'Living room,' Kumkum always corrects her. Now she keeps silent.

'What did that bastard do to you, Kumkum? What happened to your hair?'

"OK!' Kumkum stops her with a hand held up. 'OK,' she says again. 'Anya. I have never known a girl like you. You think you can fix me, fix everything. But sometimes you can't.'

'What are you talking, Kumkum?' Anya mimics Kumkum, sounding as she does when she is tired.

'You are not married. These things happen. Please.' Kumkum pulls her tin towards her. She lifts the photos and places them inside as if putting them to bed. She picks up the lid, with its picture biscuits and tartan pattern, and presses it down. She hugs it to her. 'Nunni and me ate all the biscuits before she left for school,' she says. She bends her head. Her shoulders shake with effort. Her tears catch on the tin, it feels cool against her forehead. When she looks up again, Anya is gone.

Kumkum still sits in the kitchen. Particles of dusk seem to collect around her like lazy flies; the sharp-edged autumn is coming. Her hands, usually busy with cooking or stitching or cleaning, are still. Her chunni is in place on her head and in front of her the tin is closed.

Shalu's car pulls into the drive. The lights flick Kumkum's face with a cursory glance and then go out. She hears the car door slam, and yet the gas is not lit to cook his evening meal, the rice soaks cold on the draining board, the subji remains uncut. 'Kumkum!' shouts Shalu as he comes through the screen door. His voice has a whisky marinade.

Kumkum snatches up the tin. She stands and turns, scraping the chair on the floor then steadying it. The stool is still beneath the cupboard, she climbs and replaces the tin. And then, she only has time to straighten the curtain and place the mandir tray on the table, light a candle start her prayers, before Shalu puts his head around the kitchen corner. He watches her: she hears him sniff loudly then leave. But under the wide eyes of Lakshmi Devi, all six of her arms bearing weapons as if to chop to pieces her white plastic frame, Kumkum's mind remains utterly blank. Between her palms there is nothing, only a slick of sweat.

After ten minutes, when she can hear the water running into the bucket for Shalu's bath, she wipes her hands on her sari and places the mandir carefully back on the top of the cupboard. Stepping down from the stool she snaps on the light, which only deepens the gloom. Against the gulp of the jug and the splash of his pani, she begins to prepare the dinner. She serves it to Shalu, who does not look up from his Times of India. He eats. He reads. At last he is finished. He folds his paper and rises from his chair. With her back to him she can still see him as he is every night. Stretching and turning from the kitchen. Going to wash his hands and mouth, clear his nasal passage. She reaches for his whisky. She will place it with a glass next to his chair inside. She reaches up, and from behind her husband's hand grips her wrist.

'Where is Anya?' he shakes her.

'Let me go, Shalu, I don't know where Anya is. Gone out.'

Shalu does not let go. 'Where is she, Kumkum? Usually she tells you what all she is doing.'

Kumkum tries to pull her arm down but Shalu raises it higher and grips her tighter.

'Kumkum I don't want trouble if she has run off with some boy. And her rent is supposed to be coming today. Now, where is she?'

'Rent is paid, this morning, Ji. I don't know where she is.' She twists her neck and looks her husband in the eye. She can see the veins, carrying his lifeblood, bulging at his temples; the deep creases where he smiles at everyone like he is the best friend of the world. 'Anya is not yours to tell "come in go out", only.'

Shalu lets Kumkum go. His hands hang at his sides, but he does not step back.

'Where is she?' he asks again.

'Hello.'

Shalu turns. 'Anya! Just in time for whisky, huh? Come. Please.' He gestures to the room as if she is the guest he has been waiting for all his life. 'Kumkum, bring our glasses in the main room. Come, Anya, come.'

Kumkum's hand does not shake but her eyes go to Anya's face. Anya has already turned. She is following Shalu into the other room. Kumkum loads the tray with glasses and nuts and ice and the whisky bottle. She takes it in after them, places it in her husband's reach and retreats to crouch on the dark part of the stairs where she can hear, and not be seen.

'So Anya, how do you like your whisky tonight? Strong, hain?' This is Shalu's opening line. Kumkum rubs her wrist and waits for Anya's usual answer, 'As strong as Amitabh Bachan, Shalu, as strong as you.' Usually it makes her smile. Now she waits, breath held, to hear the Anya she knows.

'Yes. Make it strong, Shalu.' Anya's voice is soft and quiet.

No, thinks Kumkum. She sits still in the dark and does not exhale.

'Anya. Cheers.'

Two glasses clink together.

'Cheers, Shalu. So.'

'So.'

'Shalu.'

'Anya. A ha ha ha.'

Kumkum puts her hands to her cheeks. Her skin feels stretched over her face, her eyes hollow sockets in the dark. One hand unties her chunni to smooth her head.

'Would you like me to fill your glass again, Anya?'

34

Shalu always offers, Anya always makes an excuse to have water –

'Thanks Shalu, you're such a great host. But why don't you let me be hostess?' Anya's laugh cracks cold and hot like ice meeting whisky in the glass.

Kumkum's fingernails dig into her scalp. She edges up the stairs, further into the dark, until she is on a level with the kitchen cupboards and the mandir with its promising gods. On her other side, the living room wall hides Anya and Shalu from her.

'Come then Anya, fill up the glasses, and tell me what all you got up to today. I like to hear your stories you know, I'm an old man, I need your energy.'

'Not so old, Shaluji, not so much.'

Again, the clink of the glasses, the rasp of Anya's voice. Curls of Lucky Strike smoke feel their way up the stairs; ghostly fingers of it stroke Kumkum's face. Every part of her stiffens, everything is held. Again, she tries not to breathe. Anya said Shaluji.

'Yes! You are right, Anya. The wisdom of youth and beauty.' Shalu laughs. He is flattered. He believes he has won.

'Come Anya, the world turns, let's drink to time passing and help it along. Cheers!' She hears them drink and imagines : Anya's head going back, her white throat, the whisky going down. Shalu settling in, his white kurta shocking against the old blue chair. The high-watt light, casting their eyes to darkness.

'One more,' she hears Anya say. 'We are both so thirsty. And I'll tell you what I did today, Shaluji. Yes. A great story, one you will like so much.'

'Great. Yes, fill it up. A bit more. Yes! And one more ice, only. Don't you know how I like my drink yet?'

Kumkum exhales, rests her head on her knees; Shalu is drunk, already.

'OK, OK, I know. But you should have a son to drink with, and a daughter to pour your drink for you.'

'What do you mean Anya? What are you suggesting?' says Shalu.

'I went to see her today. Nunni. And I met Ashish this afternoon too. Wow, what children!'

Kumkum gets to her feet. In the dark, she stands on the stairs, steadying herself with her arms stretched out, holding herself up by pushing the walls away. Her chunni slips from her head. Nunni. She pushes harder, her body trembling.

'Ah!'

She stops. Her husband has cried out.

'What must you think, Anya! A man with two children yet all alone.'

Kumkum's arms drop to her sides. She takes a step down towards the living room. Towards them. The children.

'A man whose wife seems to be so quiet and calm, but is a danger to herself!'

A step back. Anya says something, but Kumkum cannot hear.

'A danger to her own children? Her husband? Can you imagine, Anya?'

Now her voice is disappearing into his.

'Yes!' he continues. 'Anya do you think there is any comfort for me from any of them? I sent them away to protect them! And she! Not even dinner ready when I come home at night.'

'Come, Shalu, come. Here.' Anya speaks as if sucking her own words from the air, her voice caught on the snarls of smoke still inside her throat.

'Yes,' slurs Shalu. 'You at least know when to fill a glass.'

'Poor Shalu.'

'Poor? Oh no Anya, you think this is all Shalu has?'

Is Anya smiling and nodding? Is Shalu looking at her like Ashish used to look when he pretends it was not him who ate the last jelabi from the bag? She hears a soft movement as if one person has slipped off their seat and is standing, or kneeling in front of the other.

It is Shalu. Shalu is moving. Where is Anya?

'No. Because of them, I am a rich man.'

What is he saying? There has never been enough money for meat in their house. Their house. The roof, the walls, Ashish's room, the yard, the swing, the gate. She breathes in and holds it, then again even more.

'Don't have to work either, and so I am a clever man too. You might think this place is ramshackle, but the land, Anya, the land. What do you think of that?'

Suddenly she understands how her husband can afford his black market imported red-label. In the dark she crosses her arms around her body, rubbing her chapped hands over them, feeling the fabric of her kameeze catch on her skin.

'I sold the house long time back – got to have something for later. And the land lease is promised with interest to Raviji; he needs his security also. Happy the man whose son is strong, whose daughter is well paid for, no?'

'Shalu – whatever with the house.' Anya says. 'I know. Why don't we bring them back here?'

Hearing Anya's silken question, Kumkum's eyes begin to itch, to burn.

'Who?' Shalu says. 'What do we need with anyone else, Anya? You and me, and Johnnie…I don't need any of you!'

Kumkum's arms shoot sideways again, her hands push harder on the walls, push as if she could bring the house down around their ears. She hears Shalu get up, a scuffle, a glass breaks, there is sucking sound, a slapping and Anya swears, 'Fuck!' There's a crash, and a laugh; there is silence.

Kumkum turns in the dark, and goes up the stairs to her room.

In the morning, Shalu carries on. Anya's door is closed. As the day passes, she does not come down.

Kumkum prepares a tray for her. She knocks gently on the door she used to leave open so she could hear the children in the night. She knocks harder. Then she twists the handle, and pushes. The door opens. On the ledge is the nest of painted Kashmiri boxes, one two three four five. On the mirror hangs a loop of pretty glass bangles. But Anya herself is gone, and so are her cameras, her hairbrush, her clothes.

III

From her window, Nunni can see : a web of lights thrown over the trees, bald heads and up-dos bob about underneath, they look funny. Waiters in stiff white coats hold trays of crystal glasses full of juice. She can't make out faces and she doesn't know most of the people there. But so what na, because today is her wedding day.

How many times has she practised this day? She turns away from the window and back to her hotel room, stiffly because of the weight of the wedding sari, almost blindly, because the dresser has pulled it to a low peak over her eyes. Gold marks her parting and keeps her head in the correct position. Her sari keeps slipping even with too many pins. She keeps trying to smooth her hair back, but her hand catches in the chain that links her nose stud to her earrings.

'Like a cow,' her brother said when he came to take her 'before' picture. But he didn't mean it; he was smiling as he positioned her. He took his time : the light was not right; her chin had to be lower, her eyes wider. Her body had to be straighter, her sari pleats sharper. He told her to show him her toes in their sandals; and then he told her to put them away. She knew how important it was to get it just perfect. After all, the pictures will outlast the day – so Seema Mummyji keeps telling her.

Nunni can do nothing but stand and wait. And watch. In fact, she cannot stop looking at the crowds. Outside, the barāt is arriving, and she cranes her neck to see if she can see

40

him. And then she does. Mohun. Her future, borne high on a chariot pulled by a rented pony. Through the lush gardens of the hotel, he is coming for her, to do all the things he has been promising her for the last few months. Tonight, when she takes off all of this gear; it is too much to think of.

The lights reflecting from the infinity pool give him a filmy glow. She catches her breath: yes. It is exactly like the movies that she used to watch with Seema Mummyji on Sunday afternoons, when she was a small girl. This is one goddam hundred per cent better. He is draped in flowers, surrounded by his sisters, aunts, girl cousins, his mother, even his grandmother, she can see. They dance around him, to the beat of drums: they wheel under the lights, around Mohun. He is coming for her and tonight will be here soon. She clenches her legs together. It feels like she wants to pee. Her fingers go to her mouth and she sucks for a moment on the little one.

This morning, he sent her orchids, flown in from Dubai. So waxy perfect she thought they were plastic, and disappointment lumped in her throat. She dug her nail into one petal and hurt the pad of her thumb on the other side. Then she realised the flowers were real. Wow. There was a pink box too, tied with black ribbon. So she is wearing Agent Provocateur under her wedding sari. Her nipples are scooped like ice cream offerings into points in quarter cups, her chuchi is wrapped in matching lace that parts where her legs part, two tiny black pieces with the slit edged in ribbon and held together by bows. Imagining tonight, she feels as if she has escaped all of her outfit and left it standing on its own while she shows herself naked. No one should see her like this, with this smile, with this flush. She checks the mirror. The layers of pale foundation lighten her skin and hide any colour underneath.

Nunni twists off an orchid head, sails slowly to the balcony doors. She opens them and steps to the edge and leans over. As she watches, Mohun shakes a bottle of champagne and lets the cork fly, spraying his crowd in froth and fizz. They open their mouths, they tilt back their heads, they laugh. She retreats back inside, the orchid flower crushed in her patterned hand.

For hours yesterday in the dry heat of the Delhi winter, she sat in the hotel gardens while four ladies stretched out her limbs and painted her with a myth of how she and Mohun met. A God and his consort, they said. A Krishna and a Radha. A Brad and Angelina. Yes, she thought. Dark green mehndi paste turned hard on her arms, her hands, her feet, her legs. The women rubbed her with lemon to make sure the marks would take longer to fade; she almost wanted it to sting, she was numb with the boredom of watching everyone else have fun. Now she can see the painted Mohun and the Nunni, they kiss when she puts her palms together.

A knock on the door. She slowly crosses to open it. Madhu, in her bridesmaid's blue and gold. The cousins face each other and Nunni takes a deep breath. She steps a bit forward, and stands on the threshold.

'Holy fuck, Nunni, you look amazing!' Madhu reaches out her arm as if she is going to catch the end of Nunni's wedding sari, pull it off her and stuff it in her mouth. 'Let me see your mehndi?' her cousin asks, and Nunni holds out her hands. 'It's sort of rusty looking, isn't it? Like dried blood,' says Madhu grinning. 'Very Twilight. Remember–'

Nunni takes a step forward and faces Madhu without replying.

Madhu straightens into solemnity. She puts one hand on Nunni's arm and the other on her shoulder. They begin down the hotel corridor, carpets muffling the clack of their heels, muzak blending with the chink of wedding bangles, take the marble steps and walk through the shining lobby, where their clack and chink now reach the tourists and businessmen, who stare and point and take photographs, measuring and marking them for grace and beauty and form as they make their way towards the wedding.

All through that walk, Nunni feels Madhu's nails poking into her arm. She tries to move her shoulder, but the yoke of her necklace is too heavy, so she pulls a bit harder. That's when they get to the edge of the party, and that's when her sari gets caught in Madhu's bangles.

The threads of silk pull and pucker the fabric into wrinkles. The two girls stop, frozen. Nunni can see : Ashish's grin, but not his eyes, his camera is pointed at her. There is his blondie girlfriend next to him – 'Angrezi Barbie,' Madhu calls her when she wants to be mean. Someone tries to push her gently forwards. The groom's group is waiting. She has to get free.

Madhu's father is suddenly beside her, trying to pull her from Madhu, trying to elbow Madhu out of his way. 'Come on!' Vivek Uncle hisses through his smiling teeth; 'You girls have kept them waiting too long. It looks bad!'

'Papa!' whispers Madhu, 'My bangle is caught!'

Nunni can hear them on either side of her, and feels unable to move. She watches her shadow spill across the ground towards her husband-to-be. Don't move, she thinks, and then feels a jerk and a pull of fabric over her breasts, and puts her hand to her throat, sure that her skin is suddenly aging on fast-forward. There is a flash as Ashish captures her like this : hand on heart as if stopped, people will say when they see the photograph, by sheer love before the mandir.

Vivek Uncle takes over and Nunni walks in his grip. He only lets go when she is in position, facing Mohun. A thin red thread runs from the silk on her shoulder; she is still caught on Madhu's bangle. She moves her head slightly to the right. She sees a crowd of silk and jewels, some turned towards her, most turned away. On her left : Ravi Papaji and Seema Mummyji sit on low stools, opposite Mohun's parents. They are not looking at her. Between them a fire, waiting to be lit. She turns back to face Mohun. Someone puts a garland in her hands. St Michael, she whispers to herself. Her childhood mantra.

She dips her head. Mohun places a flower necklace around her neck. The thread connecting her and Madhu snaps and its two ends float aimlessly in the air, the ropes of a swing with no one on the seat. Nunni reaches up and places her garland around Mohun's neck. They sit to be married. They stand, and are tied together. They walk around the fire. Again circle, again circle, again circle, again circle, again circle, again circle – turn – circle, again circle, again circle, again circle, again circle, again circle, again circle – stop. They do as commanded by the pundit, who speaks in Sanskrit and English so everyone – from the Indian family to Mohun and Nunni's Angrezi friends, all dressed up in borrowed saris and turbans for the evening – can understand.

The smoke from the fire obscures her view. Petals swarm towards her from the crowd. Nunni looks up to see her father leaning sideways, smiling, smiling; she does not need to see the whisky bottle hidden under his chair. There is her Seema Mummyji and Ravi Daddyji, Kiran Aunty and Vivek Uncle, her brother and Angrezi Barbie beside him. And Madhu. Your turn next, Nunni's eyes promise Madhu, but she seems to be frozen, staring at Nunni as if she does not recognise her. Nunni wants to laugh but she cannot move her neck.

Everyone else looks relieved, as if they all have successfully finished some important task. What have they done? Nunni's mouth dries out and she searches the crowd of faces, looking for someone who can see everything more clearly than she can, than she has ever been able to. The huge hired spotlights are more blinding than the sun. Hundreds of eyes stare at her and she can't breathe, dizzy as if she is seeing everything from a height. Her gaze sweeps the crowd and now takes in Mohun's mother and father. His sister, his brother. They do not look relieved, they look expectant and ready, as if there is a huge task they have to begin straight away. What is it?

And then sensation returns to her body with the dead weight of Mohun's arm around her shoulders. As much as she can, she raises her eyes and bends her neck back. He is smiling at the crowd. She realises she cannot shift him off her. A noise rings in her head, honest and insistent as an old cowbell doing battle with the car horns in the Delhi traffic.

Acknowledgements

This book belongs to:

Meera Taneja.

My heartfelt thanks are due to all at Gatehouse Press for selecting my story and producing it so beautifully, in particular Sam Ruddock, Andrew McDonnell, Julia Webb and Meirion Jordan.

Thank you Ben Crowe, Emily Evans, Pria Doogan, Sophie Gilmartin, Kristen Harrison, Sophie Mayer, Juliet Mitchell, Andrew Motion, SF Said, Neelam Taneja, Eley Williams. To all the writers who contribute each day to *Visual Verse*, thank you.